The Ideal Home

Stories linking with the History
National Curriculum Key Stage 2.

To Bronwen Mills, who told me
the story of the wind.

First published in 1999 by Franklin Watts
96 Leonard Street, London EC2A 4XD

Text © Elizabeth Buchanan 1999
Illustrations © Kate Sheppard 1999

Editor: Claire Berridge
Designer: Jason Anscomb
Consultant: Dr Anne Millard, BA Hons, Dip Ed, PhD

A CIP catalogue record for this book
is available from the British Library.

ISBN 0 7496 3361 1 (hbk)
     0 7496 3553 3 (pbk)

Dewey Classification 942.081

Printed in Great Britain

CROSS N.S

The Ideal Home

by Elizabeth Buchanan

Illustrations by Kate Sheppard

W
FRANKLIN WATTS
NEW YORK • LONDON • SYDNEY

1

A chance encounter

It was the kind of Sunday morning that
seems to go on forever. The sun
shimmered out of the hazy sky, and
glistened on the puddles and pools left by
the showers of the day before. The
windows of the close-packed buildings had

been thrown wide open to catch a breath of cool air, and conversations drifted down and mingled to a gentle hum.

Anna ran down the narrow street, followed by Peter, rolling his hoop. From time to time she looked back over her shoulder to make sure she wasn't too far ahead. They were both learning to control the hoop along the uneven streets and lanes, knocking it along with the short stick.

Peter wasn't catching her up, but nor was he so far behind that she would have to stop and wait. She glanced back again as she rounded the corner, and ran, full tilt, into a well-dressed gentleman, burying her nose in the rough cushion of his stomach.

"Oh, sir! Oh, sir!" Anna, out of breath and startled, could barely speak. "I'm sorry, sir!" She got no further.

Around the bend came Peter, straight into Anna. The gentleman had seen Peter in time to hold out his arms to support both children. The hoop rolled ahead and clattered down onto the cobbles.

The gentleman let go and looked down on the two children.

"I'm Mr. Cadbury," he said gravely. "I am delighted to meet you both!" His eyes were merry, and there was now mud on his fine trousers.

Peter and Anna stood up straight.

"I'm Peter Ind, sir," said Peter, "and this is my friend, Anna Lewis."

Anna smiled. "I

think my father knows you, sir, from his Adult School Class, that he goes to after church on Sunday morning."

Mr. Cadbury nodded. "Mr. Lewis does come to my Sunday morning class," he agreed. "I saw him this morning. He is a fine man, and I am pleased to meet another member of the family. Now, let me walk you both home. It's late enough and your families will be wondering if you're ever coming in to eat!"

Taking up the hoop, he set off down the street with the children.

Their home was a tall old building. Peter's family rented rooms on the top floor, up three flights of stairs; Anna's family had rooms on the floor beneath. The building was shabby, and the bricks were black from the smoke of coal fires and the fumes of the surrounding factories.

They entered the back courtyard, which

was shadowed by the nearby buildings. Anna suddenly felt embarrassed and fell silent. It always smelt here, even more than in the street. Each family emptied the contents of their chamber pots and pails into the gutters. It never got rinsed away thoroughly. Mr. Cadbury and Peter chatted on, ignoring the stench.

"Anna and I are making it, and when it's ready, we'll all go on a tram with my father and we'll find a hill to fly it!"

When Peter was excited, he shared his enthusiasm with everyone. He and Anna had been planning a kite for weeks and, finally, Anna's father had brought home some leftover bits of wood from work, which were ideal for the framework.

Mr. Cadbury and

Peter discussed design and size, but when they came to talk about building methods, Anna forgot her embarrassment, and joined in. When Mr. Cadbury said goodbye and turned away, both children were sorry to see him go.

"I'll be watching the hills for that kite!" he called as he left the courtyard.

2

Starting the kite

The children hurried to the pump, where a good splash removed the mud from their hands. They rubbed their faces, too, and dried themselves on their handkerchiefs.

There was the smell of cooking on every floor as they pounded up the

staircase. Peter's older brothers and sisters
might be late, but Anna knew that her
family would be on time. She could hear
her brother Harry's cough, even before she
reached the door.

They were all waiting for her: her
parents, her twelve year old brother Tom,
and the little ones, Frank and Harry.

"There you are!" exclaimed Pa. "I thought I'd be seeing you on the way home from class. What's kept you this morning?"

"We almost did meet you," explained Anna. "We were on our way, and then we bumped into the teacher – your Mr. Cadbury. We got him muddy, I'm afraid, and he walked us home."

Mother sighed. "You don't always make the best impression, Anna! Behaving like a young scamp in front of a gentleman!"

"It was all very respectable, Mother," protested Anna. "And Mr. Cadbury said he was delighted to meet us!"

"There's no accounting for some tastes!" murmured Tom in the background, and Anna grinned as she sat herself down beside him.

Mother served the steamed pudding first, to take the edge off their hunger. Then spring greens and potato with a scrap of meat. This was the best meal of the week and they savoured it, the children eating quietly, while Pa talked about his class, the other students and the teacher.

"We're lucky to have him," stated Pa. "He gives us so much to think about in class, but his life is an example to us, too.

He's a businessman, with a large factory to run, but he works in his spare time to help others, and make their lives better. What a conscience he has!"

That afternoon, Anna and Peter played outside in the street. In the evening, after tea, Anna gathered the scraps of fabric which her mother had given her, and took them with the wood for the kite up to

Peter's kitchen, where his family had
obligingly made room on the table for
the kite project.

Anna bent over the scraps, making a
pattern of the different colours and shapes,
while Peter trimmed the wood, and began
to lash two bits together.

Too soon, Peter's family came in.

"We should finish it by next week,"
Peter reassured Anna, as they put away
their work.

3

Changes

It was still dark when they got up on Monday morning. As usual, they were wakened by Harry's cough. It never left him, and Mother said it was because the air was so sooty, and their rooms were so damp.

Tom and Pa had filled the big water crock in the kitchen the night before, carrying buckets from the pump in the courtyard below. Now they both washed,

using the large basin, and rinsing with warm water sloshed from the jug, while Mother made the breakfast.

Anna's bed was in a curtained-off corner of her parents' bedroom. She dressed quickly, so she could help the little boys to get ready. They shared a room with Tom, and had to stay in bed until he was up, because there wasn't enough space for them all to move about in the room.

It was always an early start for working men, and Tom went off, too, to the carpenters' workshop where Pa worked and where he was an apprentice.

When they had gone, there were plenty of household chores to finish before school.

Anna did the dishes and swept the floor, while Mother emptied the pails down in the courtyard. Then Anna lugged buckets of coal up from the coalstore below.

"Race you to the landing!" she

laughed to Peter as they both struggled up the stairs together. The buckets were only

half full, but they were heavy enough for
youngsters. It took several journeys to
bring up enough coal for the day.

Peter helped Anna with the last bucket
of coal. Before he dashed off to finish
getting ready for school, Anna's mother
checked that their hands and faces were
clean. She then sent Anna and her

younger brothers out of the door to school. Before the door was shut behind them she was already threading her needle, ready to set to work on the clothes she was making for her customers.

"Peter!" shouted Frank and Harry, and Peter appeared immediately, pulling on his coat as he clumped down the stairs with Anna and her brothers.

When Anna saw Peter that evening, he wasn't thinking about the kite. "Anna, you won't believe it – we're going to move!" Anna stopped on the stairs. It didn't sound like her voice asking, "How far away?"

"Oh, miles!" answered Peter, too excited to notice her distress. "We're to live by the chocolate works. My brothers will walk to work there, and my father's going to work there, too! And, Anna, we'll live in a real house, with a garden and trees!"

Anna listened in wonder. It sounded like a fairy tale, and she smiled for Peter's happiness.

When he helped bring the bits of half-made kite down to Anna's, however, he was subdued.

"Maybe you could finish it and come and fly it near our new house?"

he suggested quietly.

Maybe she would. It was something to look forward to.

For a while after Peter moved away, Anna worked every evening on the kite. She missed Peter terribly, and not just because the kite was taking twice as long to make! There was no one to laugh with on the stairs in the morning, no one to help look after Frank and Harry on the way to

school. No one to run with her on a Sunday morning, to meet her father from class. Without Peter beside her, chattering and playing, she was aware of the dank, narrow streets, putrid and running with filth. The black and dingy houses loomed cheerlessly around her.

After school, while her schoolmates gathered outside to eat their meal of bread and lard, and to play, Anna spent more and more time on the kite, using her tiniest stitches to sew together the brightest swatches of fabric. There was plenty of black and brown for background, but any bit of colour, even if it was only a finger

wide, was added to the pattern. She was
pleased when she fitted it onto the wooden
frame. It was a beautiful kite. But there
was no room to store it like that, so she
took out the crosspiece, rolled it all
together, and put it out of the way, in the
corner by her bed. It was wintertime – too
wet and cold to fly a kite.
Pa promised that in the
spring, when the evenings
were lighter, they would
take it out on a Saturday
night, after he got
home from work. It
was going to be a
long wait.

Pa was talking
about a new housing
development to the west

of Birmingham. Mr. Cadbury was
building a model village at Bournville –
not just for the factory workers, but for
anyone. With so many new houses being
built there, they needed more carpenters.
It would mean travelling a long way to

work every day, but it was worth thinking about. In fact, the more he found out about it, the more interested Pa became.

One Sunday he announced to the children, "We're moving to the country!" His face was glowing with happiness.

"You'll go to a different school, and Tom and I will join a new workshop."

"Mother can do her dressmaking, and I'll keep chickens, and we can have an egg whenever we want one!" chimed in Tom. They each had dreams of what a new life in the country would bring.

"We'll have fruit from our own garden," put in Mother quietly, "and you children will grow up with fresh air and wholesome food. Harry may even lose his cough in all the sunshine!"

Anna swirled her four-year-old brother round with happiness, but set him down quickly when he began to cough and wheeze with excitement. She hugged him instead. There was so much to look forward to!

4

Moving day

On moving day, Mother left Pa and Tom
loading the borrowed cart, and took Anna
and the two little boys by tram to the
outskirts of Birmingham. They all had
parcels to carry to the new house in
Bournville. The tramline didn't go all the

way, and they set off down Sycamore
Road to walk the rest of the way. It was
only the heavy parcels that kept the
children from running. The parcels seemed
to get heavier and heavier, and they
walked more and more slowly.

"There's woods over there!" exclaimed
Harry, suddenly alert. "Is that where we're
going?"

"Very near," agreed Mother.

In fact, they were almost at their new

home, and before long, Mother was
saying, "This is the one!"

The houses along the road were all
different, either four in a row or two
together. Their house had a narrow
garden in the front, ready for planting.
Inside, Mother paused in the kitchen, but
Harry and Frank were already running
from room to room. Anna could hear them
upstairs, shrieking "Three bedrooms!

Three bedrooms!"

Anna was busy opening doors downstairs. There was a living-room and a large kitchen. Off the kitchen was a little room with a sink and shelves: the scullery.

But what made this small work-room special was the water tap. Anna turned it tentatively and grinned as clear, clean

water began to fill the new sink. This was
something to show Mother! But Mother
had discovered something else which made
Anna stop in astonishment, for in the
middle of the kitchen floor, where nothing
had been before, sat a full-length bathtub!

Mother's cheeks were pink with pleasure.

"We'll be the cleanest family you can imagine!" she exclaimed. "And when we've bathed, the tub stands on end in the cupboard!" and she heaved the tub back into place and closed the door.

Outside were the outhouses, and a wonderful long garden.

"Well," admitted Anna, "not quite a garden yet!" but she could imagine cabbages and potatoes growing, and apple trees and roses.

Inside, Mother smoothed her hair and washed her hands. "Now it's your turn," she instructed the children.

"Wash that city grime off your hands, and

we'll have our first country meal!"

She placed one of the bundles in the
middle of the kitchen floor. Kneeling
beside it, she untied the big knot that held
it together, and folded back the cloth.
Inside was a rice pudding, which Mother
cut into large slices for each of them.
Anna ate hers slowly, and washed it
down with water from the tap. This was
the beginning of her new life.

When Pa and Tom arrived, they filled the house with furniture and laughter. In came the kitchen table, and Pa's chair.

Mother's chair was placed by the window, and her sewing basket on the floor beside it.

Tom brought an armful of Anna's things up to her new bedroom.

"You had forgotten these," he said. "We couldn't leave your kite behind!"

They unpacked the oil lamps carefully.

"I'll put these on the window-sill for decoration, shall I?" Tom asked.

Anna looked at him puzzled, but Mother laughed.

"With gas lighting in the house we won't need the lamps! And no more candles in the bedrooms, either!"

What a wonderful house!

5

A surprise friend

The next day was Saturday, and Pa and
Tom went whistling off to their new jobs,
but there was no school. Anna and her little
brothers decided to explore the woods. There
were golden wild flowers along the banks
and under the leafless trees. Shafts of

sunlight shone against the soft grey branches. Birds were singing.

"It's a castle of silver and gold!" marvelled Anna.

"I'm going to build my den in that gold corner there!" announced Frank, and he began to roll bits of wood against two large trees bathed in sunlight.

Soon they were all building. Harry pushed a thin, curly twig into position.

"That's for the gas light," he explained.
They giggled. Even the dens in
Bournville had gas lamps!

"Anna!!"
Anna recognised the voice before she
saw who had called her. So did Harry and
Frank, and they flew across the clearing.
"Peter! It's Peter!"
"Have you moved to Bournville?"

asked Anna in amazement.

"Of course! I told you we were moving near my brothers' work: Cadbury's chocolate is made here in Bournville. When the wind is in the right direction, Bournville smells of chocolate!"

"We moved yesterday," interrupted Harry. "Will you come and see our new house? And shall we go to school together on Monday?"

Chattering, interrupting and skipping with pleasure, they escorted Peter home in triumph.

6

Bournville days

School was in the nearby town of
Stirchley, and with Peter to accompany
them, they settled in quickly. After school
they helped Pa in the garden, and soon
the trees they had planted had green
leaves opening. Harry's cough

disappeared, and in the morning they
woke to the sound of birdsong. Tom had
been promised some chicks, and began
work on a chicken house. Anna had a plot

of her own in the garden, and watched out
every day for the signs of anything coming
up in the soft brown earth.

Anna was in the garden one windy morning when Peter came to collect them for school. As she wasn't ready the boys went on ahead without her. Anna washed her hands and hurried to catch up with the others, but she could only walk slowly, struggling against the strong wind. When she tried to cross the Recreation Field, a sudden gust blew her over, and she burst into tears of frustration. All the strength of the wind was against her.

"What's all this? What's happened to you, young miss?" asked a voice above her.

Anna looked up to see Mr. Cadbury.

"I'm going to Stirchley school, sir," sobbed Anna, "but the wind is trying to

blow me back to Bournville!"

"I can help you push against that
wind!" said Mr. Cadbury. "Once we start
moving, we'll be there in no time."

He helped her to her feet, and they
started off.

"I believe we've met before!" shouted

Mr. Cadbury above the wind. "Aren't you Anna? Did you ever finish the kite you had planned?"

Anna nodded. "Yes, sir, but it's never been flown."

"A kite comes alive in the wind," mused Mr. Cadbury.

"Would you like to come along when we do fly it, sir?" asked Anna. "Would you like to launch it?"

"It would be an honour," replied Mr. Cadbury, bowing. "If the winds are good,

we can go together on Saturday afternoon."

He walked Anna to the very door of the school, and bowed again before walking away.

On Saturday, the wind was perfect for flying a kite. Anna carried the kite and Frank held its tail. Peter, Harry and Mr. Cadbury all came as well. Mr. Cadbury knew the best place to try the kite, and he led the way, the children skipping and

running to keep up with his long strides.

From the hill they looked down on the new town of Bournville.

"I can see our house!" cried Frank.

"Do you like it?" asked Mr. Cadbury

"It's a wonderful place to live!" answered the children together.

"I would like everyone in Bournville to feel that way," smiled Mr. Cadbury. "It is my fondest dream."

They opened up the kite and fitted in
the crosspiece. Only Anna had seen it like
this. There was a silence as the others took
in the splendid colours and the pattern.

"It's beautiful!" exclaimed Peter to
Anna. "I never dreamt of a kite so
glorious!"

"You've taken the time to make something very special," said Mr. Cadbury. "The design is full of brightness, beauty and splendour."

He took up the kite and Anna ran into the wind. Mr. Cadbury gave the kite a push and suddenly it was flying! Higher and higher it went, glowing in the sunshine. Peter took a turn, and the kite leapt higher still. Harry and Frank shouted with delight and raced to and fro beneath it.

Mr. Cadbury watched for a moment, smiling broadly.

"It fills me with joy to see your kite, dancing with such glee above the village of my dreams!" he said quietly.

And they filled their lungs with the wind, and went racing across the hill to take another turn with the kite.

Notes

Bournville

For over 50 years, the Cadbury family had sold tea, coffee and cocoa in Birmingham. In 1861, Richard and George Cadbury took over the business from their father. Using a new machine from Holland, they improved the recipe for their chocolate.

The business expanded until the factory in Birmingham was not large enough to cope with the demand for chocolate. In 1879, the Cadbury brothers opened a new factory (or works) outside Birmingham, with room to expand, access to the canals and railway and a fresh water supply. The water came

from a stream called the
Bourn, and the Cadbury
brothers named the area
Bournville. ('Ville' is the
French word for town.)
Everything French was

considered stylish at that time (including French
chocolate). A few houses were built for Cadbury
employees, but most of
the workers travelled
out by tram or train
from Birmingham.

Housing

The idea of providing
decent housing in
healthy surroundings
was not a new one.
In Yorkshire,
there was a
whole village, called Saltaire, built for the mill
workers employed by Sir Titus Salt. The houses

were sturdy, and there were allotments for rent so that residents could grow their own vegetables. W.H. Lever provided attractive and comfortable housing for his employees near Liverpool. This

village was called Port Sunlight, after the Sunlight soap that the factory made! People felt lucky to live in these model communities. Most workers at that time lived in the slums, which were crowded, dirty and unhealthy.

George Cadbury's scheme was different because he wanted to provide decent housing for any respectable workers, not just those at the Cadbury Works. He made sure that every house had a large garden. This land could not be sold off for building plots. People who lived in Bournville saved money by growing their own food in their gardens. They were generally healthier because the environment they lived in was cleaner and had better facilities, like running water in the home.

The first houses were begun in 1895. So that the community would have a variety of different sorts of people living in it, some of the Bournville houses were larger and more expensive than others.

Gradually, schools, shops, parks, and recreation facilities were built.

The Slums

Living in towns during the 19th century was more awful than we can imagine. The Industrial Revolution had brought many people from the country into the cities, to work in the factories. Sometimes three or four families had to crowd into one house. Some people lived in houses built especially for the workers.

In order to house as many people as possible, houses were built 'back to back': terrace houses sharing a back wall, as well as the side walls. As there were only windows at the front of this 'back to back' accommodation, air couldn't move around and through the rooms, so they were stuffy and damp.

Most people collected their water from wells or pumps in the street outside. The street was where the contents of the chamber pots were emptied. It was also where the children played. The water was easily contaminated by the filth in the street. The air was polluted by the smoke from the nearby factories and from the coal fires that warmed all the houses.

Because the houses were put up quickly and cheaply, they were frequently damp and squalid. Poor people did not have the time or the money to do anything about it. Towards the end of the century, things were beginning to improve, but people who lived in slum conditions grew up unhealthy, weak and puny.

Education

There were many different kinds of school in the 19th century. Children sometimes met for their lessons in the kitchen of

the teacher's house. Not all children went to school – some children started their working life at the age of four years old!

In 1870, a law was passed that made it illegal for children not to go to school. Even then, poor children usually left school when they were eleven or twelve, to start work. Sunday was the only day of the week that they didn't work, and classes were taught then so that workers could continue their education. They learned to write and to read the Bible, they had Bible discussion classes and lessons in morality and hygiene. Firms and businesses trained youngsters in the skills they needed for their craft. Some businesses, like Cadbury, gave their young workers time off to go to classes during the week, and many people went to lessons in the evening.

Sparks: Historical Adventures

ANCIENT GREECE
The Great Horse of Troy – The Trojan War
0 7496 3369 7 (hbk)   0 7496 3538 X (pbk)
The Winner's Wreath – Ancient Greek Olympics
0 7496 3368 9 (hbk)   0 7496 3555 X (pbk)

INVADERS AND SETTLERS
Viking Raiders – A Norse Attack
0 7496 3089 2 (hbk)   0 7496 3457 X (pbk)
Boudica Strikes Back – The Romans in Britain
0 7496 3366 2 (hbk)   0 7496 3546 0 (pbk)
Erik's New Home – A Viking Town
0 7496 3367 0 (hbk)   0 7496 3552 5 (pbk)
TALES OF THE ROWDY ROMANS
The Great Necklace Hunt
0 7496 2221 0 (hbk)   0 7496 2628 3 (pbk)
The Lost Legionary
0 7496 2222 9 (hbk)   0 7496 2629 1 (pbk)
The Guard Dog Geese
0 7496 2331 4 (hbk)   0 7496 2630 5 (pbk)
A Runaway Donkey
0 7496 2332 2 (hbk)   0 7496 2631 3 (pbk)

TUDORS AND STUARTS
Captain Drake's Orders – The Armada
0 7496 2556 2 (hbk)   0 7496 3121 X (pbk)
London's Burning – The Great Fire of London
0 7496 2557 0 (hbk)   0 7496 3122 8 (pbk)
Mystery at the Globe – Shakespeare's Theatre
0 7496 3096 5 (hbk)   0 7496 3449 9 (pbk)
Stranger in the Glen – Rob Roy
0 7496 2586 4 (hbk)   0 7496 3123 6 (pbk)
A Dream of Danger – The Massacre of Glencoe
0 7496 2587 2 (hbk)   0 7496 3124 4 (pbk)
A Queen's Promise – Mary Queen of Scots
0 7496 2589 9 (hbk)   0 7496 3125 2 (pbk)
Over the Sea to Skye – Bonnie Prince Charlie
0 7496 2588 0 (hbk)   0 7496 3126 0 (pbk)
Plague! – A Tudor Epidemic
0 7496 3365 4 (hbk)   0 7496 3556 8 (pbk)
TALES OF A TUDOR TEARAWAY
A Pig Called Henry
0 7496 2204 4 (hbk)   0 7496 2625 9 (pbk)
A Horse Called Deathblow
0 7496 2205 9 (hbk)   0 7496 2624 0 (pbk)
Dancing for Captain Drake
0 7496 2234 2 (hbk)   0 7496 2626 7 (pbk)
Birthdays are a Serious Business
0 7496 2235 0 (hbk)   0 7496 2627 5 (pbk)

VICTORIAN ERA
The Runaway Slave – The British Slave Trade
0 7496 3093 0 (hbk)   0 7496 3456 1 (pbk)
The Sewer Sleuth – Victorian Cholera
0 7496 2590 2 (hbk)   0 7496 3128 7 (pbk)
Convict! – Criminals Sent to Australia
0 7496 2591 0 (hbk)   0 7496 3129 5 (pbk)
An Indian Adventure – Victorian India
0 7496 3090 6 (hbk)   0 7496 3451 0 (pbk)
Farewell to Ireland – Emigration to America
0 7496 3094 9 (hbk)   0 7496 3448 0 (pbk)
The Great Hunger – Famine in Ireland
0 7496 3095 7 (hbk)   0 7496 3447 2 (pbk)
Fire Down the Pit – A Welsh Mining Disaster
0 7496 3091 4 (hbk)   0 7496 3450 2 (pbk)
Tunnel Rescue – The Great Western Railway
0 7496 3353 0 (hbk)   0 7496 3537 1 (pbk)
Kidnap on the Canal – Victorian Waterways
0 7496 3352 2 (hbk)   0 7496 3540 1 (pbk)
Dr. Barnardo's Boys – Victorian Charity
0 7496 3358 1 (hbk)   0 7496 3541 X (pbk)
The Iron Ship – Brunel's Great Britain
0 7496 3355 7 (hbk)   0 7496 3543 6 (pbk)
Bodies for Sale – Victorian Tomb-Robbers
0 7496 3364 6 (hbk)   0 7496 3539 8 (pbk)
Penny Post Boy – The Victorian Postal Service
0 7496 3362 X (hbk)   0 7496 3544 4 (pbk)
The Canal Diggers – The Manchester Ship Canal
0 7496 3356 5 (hbk)   0 7496 3545 2 (pbk)
The Tay Bridge Tragedy – A Victorian Disaster
0 7496 3354 9 (hbk)   0 7496 3547 9 (pbk)
Stop, Thief! – The Victorian Police
0 7496 3359 X (hbk)   0 7496 3548 7 (pbk)
A school for Girls – Victorian Schools
0 7496 3360 3 (hbk)   0 7496 3549 5 (pbk)
Chimney Charlie – Victorian Chimney Sweeps
0 7496 3351 4 (hbk)   0 7496 3551 7 (pbk)
Down the Drain – Victorian Sewers
0 7496 3357 3 (hbk)   0 7496 3550 9 (pbk)
The Ideal Home – A Victorian New Town
0 7496 3361 1 (hbk)   0 7496 3553 3 (pbk)
Stage Struck – Victorian Music Hall
0 7496 3363 8 (hbk)   0 7496 3554 1 (pbk)
TRAVELS OF A YOUNG VICTORIAN
The Golden Key
0 7496 2360 8 (hbk)   0 7496 2632 1 (pbk)
Poppy's Big Push
0 7496 2361 6 (hbk)   0 7496 2633 X (pbk)
Poppy's Secret
0 7496 2374 8 (hbk)   0 7496 2634 8 (pbk)
The Lost Treasure
0 7496 2375 6 (hbk)   0 7496 2635 6 (pbk)

20th-CENTURY HISTORY
Fight for the Vote – The Suffragettes
0 7496 3092 2 (hbk)   0 7496 3452 9 (pbk)
The Road to London – The Jarrow March
0 7496 2609 7 (hbk)   0 7496 3132 5 (pbk)
The Sandbag Secret – The Blitz
0 7496 2608 9 (hbk)   0 7496 3133 3 (pbk)
Sid's War – Evacuation
0 7496 3209 7 (hbk)   0 7496 3445 6 (pbk)
D-Day! – Wartime Adventure
0 7496 3208 9 (hbk)   0 7496 3446 4 (pbk)
The Prisoner – A Prisoner of War
0 7496 3212 7 (hbk)   0 7496 3455 3 (pbk)
Escape from Germany – Wartime Refugees
0 7496 3211 9 (hbk)   0 7496 3454 5 (pbk)
Flying Bombs – Wartime Bomb Disposal
0 7496 3210 0 (hbk)   0 7496 3453 7 (pbk)
12,000 Miles From Home – Sent to Australia
0 7496 3370 0 (hbk) 0 7496 3542 8 (pbk)